a gift for: _Carsen Feb 2013_

from: _Nana_

Copyright © 2011 Hallmark Licensing, Inc.

Published by Hallmark Gift Books,
a division of Hallmark Cards, Inc.,
Kansas City, MO 64141
Visit us on the Web at www.Hallmark.com.

Editor: Chelsea Fogleman
Art Director: Kevin Swanson
Designer: Brian Pilachowski
Production Artist: Dan Horton

ISBN: 978-1-59530-422-3
BOK1181

Printed and bound in China
JUL11

EMERSON
And the Big Soccer Tryouts

BY **Sarah Magill**

ILLUSTRATED BY **Adan Chung**

Hallmark
GIFT BOOKS

After a long journey, the trailer lumbered
to a stop. Emerson the Elephant woke
from a delightful dream about coconuts.

He was here!

Emerson looked out onto a wide

plain that looked a lot like his old home,

except the people here were louder.

They all pointed and stared, too.

Hadn't they ever seen an elephant?

"They must be pointing at my long nose," said Emerson. "Or my huge feet! Or maybe my floppy ears. I'm so embarrassed!"

So Emerson hid.

Kind of.

After a while, all the pointing,

ice-cream-cone-dropping people left.

Emerson peeked out from behind his tree.

Nobody was in sight.

"Whew!" he sighed with relief. He shook out his trunk cramps and the tingles in his toes. Then he began to look around. Soon he noticed a small round shadow by the fence.

"What's that?" Emerson asked. "Maybe it's a coconut!"

Emerson tiptoed toward the strange round thing. He gave it a trunk spin. Then he shuffled it between his huge feet. "I've never seen a coconut like this!"

"That's because it's not a coconut," chirped a voice from above. It was a friendly-looking little bird. "I thought I should tell you before you tried to eat it."

Emerson wanted to ask "What is it?" and "Who are you?" but he was too shy.

"It's a soccer ball. And I'm Ollie," the bird said anyway.

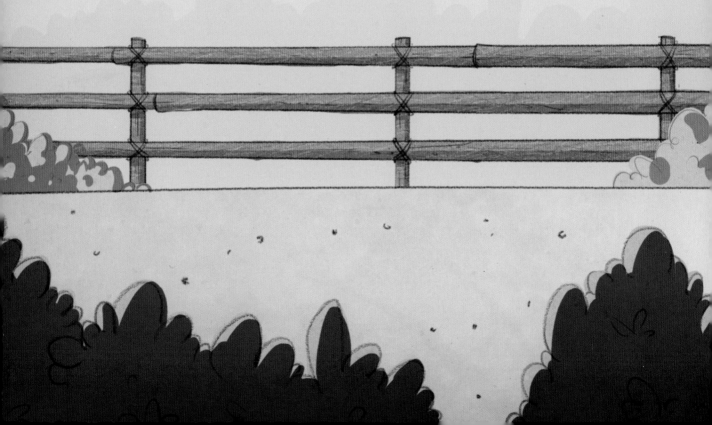

"I bet you're a good soccer player," Ollie said. "What's your name?"

"Emerson," squeaked the elephant.

"Nice to meet you, Emerson. We're having tryouts for the Zoo Cup team tomorrow. You should come!"

Emerson wasn't so sure, but before he could say so, Ollie flew off.

In the morning, the chimps pointed toward the lion's place. "That's where the soccer tryouts are!" they hooted.

Emerson was already nervous. The thought of a lion didn't help.

"Don't worry!" came a voice from above. It was Ollie. "Lynn's a nice lion. She's the coach, so she picks the team. Just remember: She's not roaring because she's mean. That's just how she talks. Come on!"

When they got to Lynn's field, it was covered with animals of every shape, color, and size. Emerson watched the players warm up. They were all wearing matching jerseys. "I'd love to have a matching jersey," Emerson whispered.

Lynn the Lion climbed onto an enormous rock and roared, "Everyone who wants to try out . . . step forrrrrwaaaaarrrrd!"

All the animals around Emerson stepped BACK.

Emerson froze.

Lynn stared before roaring, "Onto the field, then!"

Emerson was too scared to disobey. "It's just the way she talks . . . It's just the way she talks . . . " he repeated.

"DRIBBLE!"

roared Lynn.

The hyena and the fox were really good at dribbling. Emerson squished the ball by mistake.

"PASS!"

The python passed like a pro to the red panda.

Emerson's pass hit a parrot in the stands.

"HEADERS!"

The lemur, the koala and the owl bounced the ball right off their noggins into the net. Emerson's ears got in the way.

"SPRINT!"

The meerkat scampered.

The monkey bounded.

Emerson tripped over a big lizard and rolled to a stop on the sidelines.

"I'm no good," Emerson thought. "No good at all."

Lynn looked out into the crowd. "We need a goalie

for our last drill. Who will volunteeeerrrrrr?"

And before Emerson knew what was happening . . .

. . . he had volunteered.

"Thanks, Emerson!" roared Lynn. "Get out here!"

Emerson trembled. He stepped in front of the net with his eyes squeezed shut.

Then he waited.

But nothing was happening . . .

Emerson blinked one eye open.

BAM!

Emerson blocked a flying soccer ball with one swing of the trunk. "That was lucky!" he thought. But luck had nothing to do with it.

Nothing got by Emerson's long nose.

Nothing got by his big feet.

Nothing got by his floppy ears.

Nothing got by Emerson.

"I'm a goalie!" trumpeted Emerson.

"You're a goalie," chirped Ollie.

"You're ouurrrrr goalie!" roared Lynn.

That day, Emerson got a matching jersey . . .

. . . and quite a few new friends.

Did you like this story about playing soccer
and making new friends?

Please send your comments to:
Hallmark Book Feedback
P.O. Box 419034
Mail Drop 215
Kansas City, MO 64141

Or e-mail us at:
booknotes@hallmark.com